Super Sleuth
and the Bare Bones

Super Sleuth
and the Bare Bones

Super Sleuth III

Twelve Solve-It-Yourself Mysteries

■ **Jackie Vivelo** ■

G. P. Putnam's Sons ■ **New York**

Library of Congress Cataloging-in-Publication Data

Vivelo, Jackie. Super sleuth and the bare bones.
    Summary: While visiting the campus of Fenster
March College, Ellen and Beagle solve a variety of
mysteries. The reader is challenged to solve the
mysteries before Ellen and Beagle by interpreting clues
in the text.
    [1. Mystery and detective stories.   2. Literary
recreations]   I. Title.   II. Title: Super sleuth III.
III. Title: Super sleuth 3.
PZ7.V828Su   1988   [Fic]   87-7333
ISBN 0-399-21536-0

To my daughter

Contents

Super Sleuth

and the Bare Bones

.1.

An Old Mystery

I was trying to decide whether I wanted pumpkin pie, apple cinnamon cake, or caramel custard when the phone rang. I wasn't surprised to find it was my friend Beagle. Who else would interrupt Thanksgiving dinner?

"Ellen, we've got a mystery to solve. You have to come right over."

"It's Thanksgiving and all my relatives are here. I can't leave."

"Yeah, some of my relatives are here too. In fact, that's how I found out about the mystery. My aunt wants to hire the Beagle Detective Agency. I won't take the case without you."

11

As my partner in a detective agency, Beagle finds mysteries and I usually end up solving them. I have to admit he stumbles over more problems than anybody else I know. But this was Thanksgiving!

"Look, Charlie," I said, using Beagle's real name to show I was serious, "I haven't had dessert yet." Food is a major concern in Beagle's life. Missing dessert wasn't something he'd take lightly.

"Oh," he said and hesitated. "I know! Why don't you have dessert here? Ellen, this time the mystery involves a skeleton."

He hung up. I stood there strangling the receiver of the telephone, which should have been Beagle. He knows I can't resist a puzzle. Besides, we'd never had a mystery about a skeleton.

Caramel custard, that was definitely my choice. I asked Mom to put a bowl aside for me and I grabbed a jacket and headed for Beagle's house.

Charles Beaghley is the only kid my age in the neighborhood, so when he started a detective agency, he asked me to be his partner. For a while it looked like a waste of time, but now we're a pretty good team.

He must have been watching for me because he opened the door as I came up the walk.

"Aunt Irene, this is my partner Ellen Sloan," Beagle said. To me, he added, "She has a weird story to tell."

Dishes were clinking. People were talking. Somewhere music was playing. Charlie led the way to a room where we could talk.

"What has Charles already told you?" Aunt Irene asked me.

"Nothing, except that there's a mystery about a skeleton."

"I see. I guess I'd better tell you the whole story. I'm vice president at Fenster March College. We're in the middle of an extensive building program, tearing down some structures, remodeling others, and building some new ones. Last week the workmen broke through a concrete foundation at Hamilton Hall and discovered a pile of bones—human bones."

"Are the police investigating?"

"We called them at once. The police have identified the bones as belonging to a man in his late thirties. They've proved that the bones have been there as long as the building. Other evidence at the site also indicates that the body must have been put into the foundation when Hamilton Hall was built in 1890."

"What is Hamilton Hall?" I asked.

"Originally it was a residence hall for students, but

13

later it was used for offices. It's being torn down to make way for a new science building. Everyone was so excited about the building program and then these bones showed up."

"It was probably murder," Beagle said. "The skull was cracked from a blow on the head. Anyway, the body couldn't have hidden itself."

Sure it sounded like murder, but I was confused.

"Even if it was murder," I asked, "why would anybody care after a hundred years? By now the murderer is dead too."

"That's probably how the police feel, but it's a ticklish situation for the college. The last thing we want is to have our building program overshadowed by a century-old murder mystery."

"I can see the headlines now," Beagle said helpfully. "'Old Murder Dug Up at Fenster March.' 'Nightmare Bones at Liberal Arts College.' Or, how about 'The College With a Secret: Killer on Campus.'"

Aunt Irene was beginning to look faint, and no wonder! If Beagle was right, the college could be ruined by the publicity.

"What can we do to help?" I asked quickly.

"So you will help!" She smiled at us both. Looking from one to the other in the lamplight, she said, "I've heard that you two can pull answers to mysteries right out of the air. Maybe you can start by taking a look at this note."

She held up a torn sheet of paper, but before she handed it over, she explained, "Some mysterious things happened at the college in 1890. We know that four men left the college that year, and so far I haven't been able to find out what happened to any of them. At the same time, a large sum of money disappeared. The money was never found. I think it's possible that the skeleton we found may have been one of those men. Just before I left the college for the holiday, I picked up this old note, hoping it would be a clue to the mystery of the missing men and money."

"What do you want us to find out?"

"Of course I can't expect you to solve the mystery of the money or identify the skeleton from such a little bit of evidence. But if you could just tell us who 'Stoney' and 'Pop' were, I think it would be a start."

She handed us the paper and Beagle and I read together:

March 19, 1890
DEAR STONEY,
Leonard Shutt told me he had spoken to you . . .
know about the donation.

You and Martin and I would be the only ones . . .
Leonard was overheard saying "Ralph and
Pop are . . .
plan is too dangerous. I say we should just . . .

POP

When we had finished reading, Aunt Irene said, "In 1890, a large cash donation was supposed to be given to the college. Up until April of that year, the donation was a secret known only to four men. Their names were Ralph Mitchell, Leonard Shutt, James Harper, and Martin Bevis. One strange coincidence is that all four of them left the college and the community that year. Before the end of the school year a few other people knew about the gift, but these men were in on the secret from the very first. At the end of the school year, all four men and the money were gone."

"And you think this note was written by one of the four men?"

"I'm almost sure of it. At the time the note was written, they were the only ones who knew about the donation."

Using the note and the information Aunt Irene had given us, I made up a list of clues:

1. Leonard Shutt told Pop something he had already told the man called Stoney.

16

2. Martin, Stoney, and Pop were all involved in something together.
3. Leonard knew something about Ralph and Pop.

"There are too many 'somethings' in that list," Beagle said. "We don't know enough."

"If Aunt Irene is right about the group of men being the only ones to have anything to do with the donation at the time this was written, we know enough to say who Pop and Stoney are."

"How do you figure that?" Beagle asked.

"Here, I'll put what we know into a chart and you'll see what I mean."

I drew up a chart:

	Stoney	Pop
LEONARD		
RALPH		
JAMES		
MARTIN		

[Can you sort out the information and identify Stoney and Pop before you read Ellen's solution on the following page?]

Solution to "An Old Mystery":

From the first clue we learn that Leonard is neither Stoney nor Pop. The second clue tells us that Stoney is not Martin and neither is Pop. From the third clue we learn that Pop is not Ralph. Crossing off possibilities on the chart, we see that there's only one person who can be "Pop" and that is James. If James is Pop, he can't be Stoney. So Stoney must be Ralph.

"That's wonderful!" Aunt Irene said, when I had explained the answer to her. "Couldn't you two come back to Byersville with us and investigate our problems at the college?"

"Oh, I don't think so . . . ," I began, wondering what a couple of twelve-year-olds could do that the police couldn't do better.

"It would only be for this weekend. We'd drive you home on Sunday evening. Please consider it."

"Look, Ellen," Beagle said, "if they hire professional investigators, that will mean even more publicity, and publicity is what they don't want. I've spent all afternoon convincing Aunt Irene that you're a super sleuth. The least you can do is try."

"I don't know." I still hesitated. My parents know Charlie's parents, but they don't know his aunt and uncle. I wasn't sure I could go, and I wasn't sure we could help if we did go.

"You'll like the college, Ellen. The college students always treat me like I'm one of them. I'll walk back with you, and we'll ask your parents," Beagle offered. "I'll go if you can go."

After Beagle's aunt thanked us again for our help, Beagle and I started back to my house. On the way, I remembered that Charlie had forgotten the dessert he had promised me.

"You can wait in the kitchen while I get rid of my jacket. We'll eat dessert while we talk to my parents about letting me go to Byersville."

"Hi, Mrs. Sloan," Beagle greeted my mom. "Ellen invited me in for dessert."

I paused long enough to check the refrigerator and saw that the one bowl Mom had put aside for me was all that was left of the custard. Fortunately, there was still plenty of pie and cake. I told Beagle to make himself at home and went to hang up my jacket. When I got back, I found he had started without me.

"Charlie!" I gasped as the spoon disappeared into his mouth.

"Sorry, I didn't wait," he apologized. "But boy, this caramel custard is great."

.2.

A Relative Puzzle

Since Beagle had finished the last of the custard, I decided I had better settle for a piece of pumpkin pie. I got out a pie and started to cut a piece.

"I'll have one too," Beagle said. "You wouldn't want to eat alone."

While we were eating pie and telling my mother about the skeleton at Aunt Irene's college, my Aunt Amy came into the kitchen laughing.

"It doesn't make sense," she said. "Ellen, if you and Charlie can't help me, I'll give up."

"What's the problem?" Beagle asked.

"Grandmother Patterson couldn't come today, but she sent presents for all the younger kids. She sent a note with the gifts and she must think she's made it

21

clear which gift goes to which child, but it beats me."

"We just solved a problem for my aunt," Beagle said, "so it's only fair to solve one for Ellen's aunt. Where is the note?"

Beagle is always sure we can solve anything, even before he looks at the evidence. I like to see the evidence first. Aunt Amy handed us a slip of paper.

The note that came with the gifts said, "Please give these to Sherry, Gordon, Susan, and Adam."

"I'm sorry, Aunt Amy," I said. "I think Beagle agreed to help too quickly. This doesn't give us any clues."

"Now wait a minute," Beagle said. "*You* give up too fast. Maybe Grandmother Patterson doesn't care who gets which present," he suggested hopefully.

"Oh, I know she cares. She even told me to be sure that Gordon gets to play with the game even though it isn't his present."

"Well, you see," Beagle said triumphantly to me. "That's a clue."

"You're right. It is. If we can come up with a few more, maybe we can figure this out after all."

I got out my notebook and wrote down the first clue. Then I asked Aunt Amy to name the gifts.

"Let me see. The gifts are chocolate candy, a board game, a deck of cards, and a puzzle."

"Who else would Grandmother Patterson have talked to?" Beagle asked.

"I know she called Ellen's mother and she may have talked to Lillian."

Beagle and I quickly turned to my mother and asked her if Grandmother had mentioned the presents on the phone.

Mother remembered that Grandmother had said she hoped Gordon wouldn't mind not getting candy this time.

Next, we went in search of my Aunt Lillian, who is Adam's mother. Aunt Lillian said that Grandmother had mentioned that she knows Adam doesn't like chocolate candy or puzzles.

"So she wouldn't send him either of those things," she concluded.

Hearing the discussion, Uncle Cal volunteered, "She told me she thought Adam and Susan would enjoy playing with the game even though she wasn't giving it to them."

"So what do we have?" Beagle asked.

I showed him the list of clues:

1. Gordon should be allowed to play with the game although it is someone else's present.
2. Grandmother didn't want Gordon to mind that he wasn't getting candy.
3. Adam wouldn't receive either chocolate candy or a puzzle.
4. Both Adam and Susan might enjoy the game, but it wasn't a present for either of them.

"Let's see if that will do it," I said hopefully. I drew up a chart like this just below the clues:

	candy	game	cards	puzzle
GORDON				
SHERRY				
SUSAN				
ADAM				

"Now, if only we have enough information," I told Beagle. "Let's check out the possibilities."

[Can you match the children with their presents? Remember that when you have identified a gift for one child, you can eliminate that gift for the other children. When you have solved the problem for yourself, check your answer against Ellen's on the next page.]

Solution to "A Relative Puzzle":

From clues 1 and 4, we learn that the game does not belong to Gordon, Adam, or Susan. Therefore the game must be for Sherry. According to clue 2, Gordon did not get candy, and clue 3 tells us that Adam didn't get candy. Since the game was Sherry's, we know she did not get the candy. The candy must be Susan's. Now only the cards and puzzle are left. We know from clue 3 that Adam did not get the puzzle. So the puzzle must be for Gordon. The cards, therefore, are Adam's present.

"You see," Beagle said, when I had finished explaining to Aunt Amy, "that was no trouble at all."

"Thank you both," she said. "I'm sure you have helped us avoid arguments. You really are good at this detective work."

While we had been collecting clues for Aunt Amy, Beagle's Aunt Irene had called to ask Mom and Dad to let me go back to the college with them. She must have been very persuasive because they had decided to let me go.

"That's great!" Beagle told them and thanked my mom again for dessert. He reminded her that he and I had missed dessert at his house. "It's probably all gone by now, so you saved my Thanksgiving," he said.

Mom cut him a piece of apple cinnamon cake to take home with him.

.3.

Ellen's
Ghost Story

On Friday, Beagle's Aunt Irene and Uncle Doug picked me up at my house. I climbed into the back of their station wagon with Beagle and his six-year-old twin cousins, Lori and Megan.

"I'm afraid it's a two-hour drive," Aunt Irene apologized to us. "Girls, don't make pests of yourselves," she urged the twins.

"Don't worry about us," Beagle said. "We're going to tell stories."

"I like stories," Megan said.

"Me, too," Lori agreed. "What's the story about?"

"Ask Ellen," Beagle said. "She's going to tell the first one. What's the story about?"

"Me? It's your idea. You should tell a story."

27

"I will, but you start."

Beagle has great ideas, but sometimes he thinks that's all he needs to do. *He* has the idea. *I* have to do something about it.

"What kind of story would you like?" I asked.

"A ghost story!" everybody said at once.

"Okay, let me think."

"No fair," Megan said.

"Right," Beagle agreed. "These have to be 'no thought' stories."

"Okay," I said reluctantly. "Once upon a time there were four bank robbers."

"What were their names?" Lori asked.

"Oh, uh, they were called . . . Well, one was called Kirk. And—I know. Why don't you tell me names for the others. You first, Lori."

Lori squeezed her eyes shut and thought.

Good, I thought. *Maybe I'll have time to make up a story while they think up names.*

But right away she opened her eyes and said, "One was named Reilly."

"Reilly?" I asked, surprised.

"Yes," she said.

"Okay, Megan, how about a name?"

"Mine is called Duke."

"And mine is Melvin," Beagle offered without being asked.

I got out the notebook I always carry for writing down clues and found a blank page to write down the bank robbers' names.

"Now these four robbers," I said, glancing at the page, "Melvin, Duke, Reilly, and Kirk decided to rob the Dawson City Bank."

"I thought this was a ghost story," Megan complained.

"It will be," I promised. "Just wait."

"So what happened next?" Beagle prompted.

"They made very careful plans for their robbery. They watched the bank every day for a week. They drew up plans of the bank and they decided on everything they were going to do. Then one night the leader decided they were ready."

"Which one was the leader?" Lori interrupted.

"Oh, I don't know." I glanced at my list of names and said, "I think Kirk was the leader."

"No, I want Reilly to be the leader," Lori said.

"Duke should be the leader. He sounds like a leader," Megan argued.

"Okay, okay. Let's not say who the leader of the gang was. We'll work that out in a few minutes."

29

"This story is taking a long time," Beagle said.

I gave him a dirty look and tried again. "Anyway, Melvin, Duke, Reilly, and Kirk decided to rob the bank the very next night. In the middle of the robbery, the police came. The leader pulled out a gun and fired at the police, but he missed. The police fired back and one of the robbers was shot."

"Which one?" Megan demanded.

Without thinking, I said, "Duke. Duke is the one who was killed."

"Not Duke!" she wailed.

"Okay then, Melvin," I substituted.

"No way," Beagle interrupted. "Melvin would not get shot."

"It's just a story," I said. "Or it would be if you'd let me tell it."

"How do you know who got shot?" Lori asked.

"All right, let's say I don't know. Just let me finish the story and then we'll decide who's who."

They all agreed and I went on. "Three of the bank robbers escaped and went to a cabin in the woods that was their hideout. Late in the night, Duke woke the leader up to tell him he had seen a ghost, the ghost of the fourth bank robber. So the leader told Duke not to be stupid. 'Go back to sleep,' he said. In a few minutes someone else woke the leader. This time it was Reilly, who said the ghost of the fourth bank robber had stood by his bed and said, 'Give up the money.'"

Even though I was telling the story in the daytime, all the time I was talking the sky kept getting darker and stormier-looking. When I told about the ghost speaking, I said "Give—up—the—money" in a deep, spooky voice and the twins screamed.

"Well, Reilly didn't want to go back to his room, even though the leader just laughed at him and sent him away. So he went to Duke's room. He tried to ask Duke if he could sleep in his room, but before he could say anything, Duke started screaming. 'Get out of here,' he yelled, thinking the figure by his bed was the ghost. 'Go to Melvin's room. Go tell Melvin your problems.'

"Not knowing that Duke thought he was a ghost, Reilly answered, 'I tried that, but he sent me here.'

"At that, Duke jumped out of bed and rushed back to the leader's room. 'I'm not keeping that ghost,' he said, 'and you're not keeping the money.' With that, he grabbed the money, raced out to the getaway car and drove to the police station to turn himself in. And that's the story."

"Now tell us which one was the ghost and which one was the leader," Lori begged.

"Actually, I've already told you."

"No, you didn't," they answered.

"Sure I did. Look at the clues."

With Lori on one side and Megan on the other watching me write, I listed the facts I had given them:

1. Duke saw a ghost and told the leader.
2. The ghost spoke to Reilly and Reilly told the leader what the ghost had said.
3. When Duke thought Reilly was the ghost, he told him to go haunt Melvin.

"But that doesn't say who's the ghost," Lori said.

"Or who's the leader," Megan added.

"Sure it does. Let's work it out together."

I drew up a chart for the clues:

	leader	ghost
MELVIN		
DUKE		
KIRK		
REILLY		

"Put an X beside the name of any person you know for sure isn't the ghost or the leader. Then see who's left. Of course, the leader wasn't the ghost since the leader was sleeping at the cabin with the other two," I told them.

I gave them my pencil and read through the clues again slowly.

[Can you solve this puzzle? Check your answer against the solution Lori and Megan find with Ellen's help.]

Solution to "Ellen's Ghost Story":

According to the first clue, Duke is not the leader or the ghost. Reilly is eliminated as the leader and the ghost by clue 2. The third clue shows that Melvin is not the ghost, so Kirk must be the ghost. Since Kirk is the ghost, he can't be the leader. That means Melvin is the leader.

We went over the clues several times until Lori and Megan were satisfied that they had solved the puzzle.

"Hey, look at the snow," Beagle said.

The sky had been getting darker as I struggled through my story. Now snow was falling hard. For a while we watched it rush past the windows.

"How about somebody else's story?" I asked at last.

"There's won't be time now," Aunt Irene said. "We've almost reached Byersville."

.4.

The Break-In

By the time we reached Byersville, the thickly falling snow was beginning to build up.

"Maybe we'll get snowed in and you'll have to live
with us," Lori said.

"Yeah, all winter," Megan added happily.

We drove slowly through the frosty streets, past the
big old brick buildings of the college. Beside tall iron
gates, we saw a stone cougar, with red and yellow
ribbons draped around his neck, turning white under a
coating of snow.

"That statue has been there since 1870. Our college
football team is known as the Cougars. The team won
the championship this year, beating our rivals the
Hawks for the first time in three years. The ribbons

35

were hung on the statue after the game," Aunt Irene explained.

"What is that building?" I asked, pointing to a huge structure that looked very old.

"That's our administration building, the oldest building on the campus. Over to the right there you can see what's left of Hamilton Hall, the place where our skeleton was found."

"Our house is right around the corner," Megan volunteered.

"Look!" Beagle exclaimed as we turned. "Your front door is open."

"Now, what in the world—"

In seconds we were all out of the car and hurrying toward the house.

Snow was blowing in through the open door.

"The lock has been broken," Uncle Doug said. "Wait here until I check the house."

In a few moments he signaled for us to come in, and we all began to look through the house to see what was missing. The television and stereo were there. In the dining room, Aunt Irene checked for the silver.

"Nothing's disturbed upstairs," Uncle Doug said, coming down to join us.

Suddenly, Aunt Irene ran toward a room at the far end of the hall.

"All the old college records, all the information we've gathered over the past eighteen months for a history of the college, are in here."

Soon we were all six staring at a room that looked like the scene of a battle. Papers were everywhere, some crumpled, some torn.

"Oh, no!" Aunt Irene said. "It will be impossible to tell how much is missing."

Beagle and I had come to Byersville to help solve a hundred-year-old case, and now we found ourselves facing a present-day crime. Beagle was ready to take on the new problem.

"Who would steal old college junk?" he asked.

I never can resist a problem. As soon as he asked the question, I started trying to think of an answer. "Maybe there was something here somebody wanted to keep to himself."

Aunt Irene explained that the information had been sorted into boxes according to years. Beagle and I decided to begin re-sorting to see which years, if any, were missing. With so much paper in the room, it was possible someone had simply scattered things around without taking anything.

"I'm going to call the police," Uncle Doug said.

"Maybe we shouldn't touch anything until they come," I suggested.

A few minutes later, Uncle Doug came back and said to go ahead with the sorting because the police wanted to know if anything had been taken.

Aunt Irene took the twins away, and Beagle and I set to work. After a few minutes, she and Uncle Doug joined us, and we all sorted and stacked.

"It's strange," Aunt Irene said after a few minutes of sorting, "but most of the information still seems to be here."

More than two hours later, we discovered that information was missing for only one year: 1890.

"There must be some connection between this break-in and your skeleton," I said. "If the body was hidden in 1890, maybe there's something about that year that someone doesn't want us to find out."

"Ellen, I believe you're right," Aunt Irene said. "Have we picked up everything?"

"Everything except this," Beagle said, scrambling out from under the desk. "Here's one slip of paper. Hey, it's dated April 3, 1890. I think the thief either overlooked it or dropped it when he was leaving."

All of us quickly bent over the paper hoping for an important clue. The paper was headed "To All History Department Faculty."

"Let me see," Aunt Irene said, pulling a book from

one of her shelves and quickly turning pages. "In 1890, the history department consisted of five professors. They were Brandon Wells, Fred Ames, Amelia Carback, Stuart Hopewell, and Leonard Shutt. They were all here for at least a decade and took turns serving as chairman of the department."

"Leonard Shutt?" I asked. "He was one of the men who disappeared that year."

"Yes. Yes, he was. Maybe this note will tell us something."

Beagle read the memo out loud: "'Since one of our department members has been appointed treasurer of the building fund, I have asked Amelia to take on an extra class to give the treasurer some free time. The treasurer and Leonard will both represent the history department in building development meetings. Brandon, Amelia, and I will offer special reports at our next meeting. At the requests of Stuart, Leonard, and the newly-appointed treasurer, the meeting has been changed from Wednesday at 4:00 to Thursday at 4:00.' And it's signed, 'Your Chairman.'"

"I don't see what help any of that can be," Uncle Doug said.

"Well, right now, we're just collecting clues. Who knows what will help?" Aunt Irene replied.

"Maybe we should try to find out which member of the department was named treasurer of the building committee," I said.

"Yeah, if it's Leonard Shutt," Beagle said, "maybe that means he disappeared with the money."

"I think we can identify the treasurer and the chairman of the history department from this note."

"While you're doing that, I'm going to start supper," Aunt Irene said.

When she and Uncle Doug had left, Beagle and I set to work listing clues from the note:

1. The chairman asked Amelia to take an extra class to give the treasurer more free time.
2. The treasurer and Leonard both would attend building committee meetings.
3. Brandon, Amelia, and the chairman were all scheduled to deliver reports at the next meeting.
4. Stuart, Leonard, and the treasurer asked the chairman for a new meeting time.

I drew up a chart to check off the clues:

	chairman	treasurer
BRANDON		
FRED		
AMELIA		
STUART		
LEONARD		

[Can you identify the person who served as chairman of the history department and the person who served as treasurer of the building committee? You will need to identify the chairman in order to find the treasurer. When you have solved the puzzle, check your answer against Ellen's on the following page.]

Solution to "The Break-In":

The chairman is not Amelia or Brandon, according to clue 3. Also the chairman cannot be Stuart or Leonard, according to clue 4. So the chairman is Fred. Amelia is not the treasurer, as we see from clue 1, and neither is Leonard, according to clue 2. Stuart is not the treasurer, as we see from clue 4. And, we know that Fred cannot be the treasurer because he is the chairman. Therefore, the treasurer is Brandon Wells.

We reported our findings to Beagle's aunt, and we all sat down to eat supper.

"I don't see how this will help," I said.

"We've lost almost everything I had collected for that particular year," Aunt Irene said. "What you found out from that scrap of paper is a start toward building a new file for 1890."

I thought she was just being polite. I just didn't see how Beagle and I were going to be much help at all.

I didn't have long to worry about it because the twins had news of their own.

"It's still snowing," Megan said.

"And we heard on television that it's going to keep snowing all night."

"What happened to the police?" Beagle asked. "A little snow shouldn't stop them. Someone should have been here to investigate before now."

"Someone's supposed to come, but they've been delayed," Aunt Irene said, looking worried. "I was waiting until after supper to tell you. It seems they've found another body at the college."

.5.

Skeleton by Night

As soon as we recovered from our shock at the news, we all began to ask questions at once.

"Where?"

"Who was killed?"

"What happened?"

"Is it a skellington?"

The last question was asked by the twins, and they turned out to be right.

"Bones, just bones again," Uncle Doug said. "Do you know what this will do to the college?"

"This makes the headlines even better," Beagle said. "'Hamilton Hall Built over Bones.' 'How Many Skeletons Hidden at Fenster March?'"

Aunt Irene moaned. Beagle's imagination wasn't helping the situation at all.

"A quick solution would give them different head-lines," I suggested. "How about 'Hundred-Year-Old Mystery Solved at Fenster March'?"

"That would certainly be better," Aunt Irene agreed.

"I think Beagle and Ellen and I should walk over and take a look," Uncle Doug said. "Lori and Megan should go to bed," he added before they could ask to come along. After a few loud protests from the twins, it was settled. Bundled in coats and scarves, we set off on the two-block walk to the campus.

"I can't wait to go to college," Beagle said. "You get to choose when you have your classes. I met one guy who said he only takes courses that meet between eleven in the morning and two in the afternoon. So far he has had breadmaking, playing the flute, geography of Asia, and stuff like that, but at least he never has to miss breakfast."

Even through the falling snow we could see the floodlights that were trained on the ruins of a building that was being torn down.

"Here's the college president," Uncle Doug said. "Maybe he can tell us what has happened."

The president nodded to us when we were introduced.

"Two skeletons in the foundation of one building! What could have happened here? Since it was so long ago, we may never know, but the scandal could ruin Fenster March. Our only hope is to find some answers before the students get back."

"Were the skeletons put there at the same time?" Beagle asked.

"I don't know," the president said, "but they couldn't have been hidden there after the foundation was poured."

"Whatever happened here," Uncle Doug said, "happened between the time the foundation was dug and the concrete was poured, a matter of a few weeks in the spring of 1890."

The president looked just as upset as Aunt Irene had been. While Uncle Doug questioned him, Beagle and I began to look around.

"You see," Beagle said, as we walked away, "even the president wants our help."

"Charlie, he is so upset he probably didn't realize he was talking to twelve-year-olds. How do you expect us to help these people?"

"If it's a mystery, we can solve it," Beagle said.

"Aunt Irene is right. This is going to be in all the papers. Do you know how famous we'll be?"

I had a feeling we'd be famous all right. My guess was that we were going to be the campus joke. Still, I followed Beagle over to take a look at the skeleton and began to listen to the conversations around us.

We soon learned that the police, checking through the rubble where the first bones had been found, had discovered the second skeleton. They had been hoping for clues to the first mystery and instead had found a second mystery.

One of the bystanders told us that at least this time a few items had been found along with the bones: a belt buckle, some buttons, a knife, and the nails from a pair of boots.

Ropes strung between poles around the old building kept the onlookers back from the place where the skeletons had been found. Around us were tall, old buildings and the blackness of a stormy night. Even the bright lights seemed eerie as they shone through the falling snow. Looking at the skeleton, I shivered and wondered how we'd ever solve this mystery. Beagle and I were still standing and watching when we heard his uncle calling us.

"Charlie! Ellen! Here's a problem that's right in

your line. Do you think you could help the president?"

"Sure," Beagle said, confident as always.

"A group of students were here earlier watching the police. Although they were supposed to stay behind the ropes, someone seems to have gotten through. The pocketknife found with the second skeleton has been taken."

"Do you know who those students were?" Beagle asked the college president as he joined us.

"Oh yes. There are only a few students here during the holiday and in any case the police collected the names of all those who were here around the time the knife disappeared. They were Keith Smith, Beth Mowser, Jill Adams, Rocky Marshall, Heather Miller, Paul Scheetz, and James Griffith. Some of them are still here."

As he told us the names, I wrote them down in my notebook.

"I'll introduce you to the ones who are still here," Uncle Doug offered.

"Come on," Beagle urged. "Let's see what we can find out."

Beagle talks to all the people he meets as though he has known them all his life. I was a little more worried about trying to interview college students.

First we ran into a girl named Beth Mowser. She introduced us to some of the others, and everybody talked to us. Beagle was right: college students are okay.

During the next half hour I forgot how cold I had been standing there by the rubble of Hamilton Hall. Beagle and I talked and asked questions, and I hurriedly wrote down all we could find out about the students who had crowded around to watch the police lay out the bones they'd found. When we had finally talked to everyone there, we had collected the following information:

1. Keith Smith, Heather Miller and someone wearing a ski mask all left before the knife was found.
2. Rocky Marshall and the person in the ski mask had come down from the dorm on sleds. James Griffith and Beth Mowser had joined them at the foot of the hill.
3. James Griffith told Beth Mowser that he had seen the knife stolen, but he wouldn't tell who took it.
4. Jill Adams said the person in the ski mask asked her to go sledding.

49

5. James Griffith said that Jill Adams had also seen the thief, but she claimed that although she had been standing by James, she had not seen anyone take the knife.

"With these clues, we can work out the truth for ourselves," I told Beagle. Then I drew a chart below the clues:

	person in ski mask	*thief*
KEITH SMITH		
BETH MOWSER		
JILL ADAMS		
ROCKY MARSHALL		
HEATHER MILLER		
PAUL SCHEETZ		
JAMES GRIFFITH		

[Can you work out the identity of the thief? Note that the person who took the knife is not the person in the ski mask since that person left before the knife had even been found. First find and eliminate the one in the ski mask, and then you should be able to tell which of the seven students took the knife. When you have come to your conclusion, check your answers against Ellen and Beagle's on the next page.]

Solution to "Skeleton by Night":

The first clue eliminates Keith Smith and Heather Miller as either the person in the ski mask or the thief. Rocky Marshall is not the person in the ski mask and neither is James Griffith or Beth Mowser (clue 2). Clue 4 reveals that Jill Adams is not the person in the ski mask. The only student who could have been the person in the ski mask is Paul Scheetz. Now we have eliminated Keith Smith, Heather Miller, and Paul Scheetz as the thief. Clue 3 also lets us eliminate James Griffith and Beth Mowser. And Jill Adams is eliminated by clue 5. Therefore, Rocky Marshall must be the one who took the knife.

When we confronted James Griffith with what we had figured out, he confirmed it.

"But I don't think he meant any harm. He must have had a reason for taking it," he said, defending his friend.

While the president reported our conclusion to the police, Uncle Doug said, "Rocky Marshall has been very interested in the college's past. He asked questions of the townspeople and collected information for the history that's going to be written. He even volunteered to help sort some of the papers, but Irene insisted on doing that herself. My bet is that he's trying to do some detective work on his own."

Walking home, Beagle said, "We're off to a good start. We've solved one crime already."

Finding out who had taken the knife, however, did not make me think we could solve the other mysteries. When I had been at home, the idea of visiting a college and investigating a mystery about a skeleton had seemed like fun. Now that we were here, especially after seeing the bones, it seemed scary.

"This time you've really done it, Beagle. Two skeletons, a break-in, somebody stealing evidence! We have old crimes, new crimes, crimes happening right in front of us. How are we supposed to handle this? Your aunt and the president are really worried."

I have to admit that Beagle looked as concerned as he can look.

"This is a tough case all right. But don't give up, Ellen. It's not just Fenster March's reputation that depends on us. You see, when we found out who took the knife, I promised the president that the Beagle Detective Agency would have the whole thing cleared up by the time the students come back."

.6.

The Missing Cougar

"**S**he's a skellington."

"No, she's not. That's silly."

"Well, she won't wake up. Let's put the sheet over her head."

"Let me try."

"You can't wake her either."

Of course, by that time I wasn't asleep. I opened my eyes to find Megan and Lori both sitting on top of me and staring down at me.

"We thought you were a ghost."

"Yeah, we tried and tried to wake you."

"What time is it?"

"Eight-twelve." "Two o'clock." They both answered.

"What were you two trying to do?" I asked.

"We're detectives, just like you and Charlie," Lori said. Or maybe it was Megan. I hadn't gotten a good look at them yet.

"And we're looking for people to detect," her sister added.

"Beagle and I don't go around investigating sleeping people. Why don't you try detecting when breakfast will be ready?"

"Mom and Dad have gone out. Beagle told us to wake you up."

"Well, you did a good job. How about getting off me so I can get up?"

While I was dressing, I heard on the radio that five inches of snow had fallen and more was expected. Listening to travelers' warnings and predictions about icy roads, I realized that the small local police force would have its hands full taking care of current problems. A mystery from a hundred years ago, even if it did threaten the existence of the college, wouldn't be as important as accidents that were happening right now.

"Have you heard the weather report?" I asked Beagle when I found him in the kitchen mixing pancake batter.

"Maybe we'll be cut off from the rest of the world,"

he said. "This way there won't be a bunch of detectives rushing in to solve the mysteries and steal the credit."

"Beagle, I don't know how you convinced your aunt we could help, but this is ridiculous. We can't solve all these problems. The college needs help right now before classes start again."

"So everything has to be solved this weekend. This weekend is all the time we have to stay here. It works out perfectly."

Sometimes Beagle is so overconfident, he makes me furious.

"How can we solve a murder, maybe two murders, and a burglary by tomorrow?"

Beagle flipped a pancake.

"The same way we figured out who your grandmother's presents were for. We'll collect clues and we'll work with them. *You* didn't think we could match up the kids and the presents. Hey, this is ready. Let's eat."

Apart from being a little mushy in the center, the pancakes weren't really bad. Megan, Lori, Beagle, and I were eating them when we heard someone pounding on the front door. Aunt Irene and Uncle Doug were still not back, so the four of us looked at each other.

"I'll get it," Beagle offered.

A few seconds later he came into the kitchen followed by Beth Mowser, one of the college students we had met the night before.

"Good morning, Beth," I greeted her.

"Hi, Ellen, I came to see if anyone here knows about what happened at the college last night after the police left. Do you know that someone stole the cougar?"

"No!"

"Stole the cougar?"

"What happened?"

We all reacted at once and Beth sighed.

"I knew it was too much to hope that there was news already. We thought if the police knew anything about it, they would go to the president's house or here first. No one knows how it was moved, but there's a big gaping hole in the ground and the cougar is gone."

"Who did it?" I asked.

"We don't know for sure, but everybody believes the Polytech Hawks are responsible. We just took the district championship away from them for the first time in three years. That cougar is more than a symbol for the team. It's been there almost as long as the college has. If Polytech wanted revenge, this would do it."

"It's a good thing we're on the spot," Beagle said. "With a couple of century-old skeletons, a break-in, and a stolen cougar, this college needs detectives."

"We could certainly use your help in getting that cougar back. I hate to think what's going to happen when all the students get back and find out that it has been stolen. Without that statue Fenster March just wouldn't be the same."

Even though Beth said there was nothing to see but a hole in the ground, we decided to walk back with her to look for ourselves. Snow was beginning to fall again as the twins, Beth, and Beagle and I walked to where we had seen the statue the day before. Today there was a big hole two or three feet deep, with a mound of snow and rocks and dirt beside it.

"The statue must have been embedded in the soil," I guessed.

"The base used to be about four feet high. You can see how tall it was in old pictures," Beth told us. "I guess it sank into the ground over the years because now the base is only about two feet high. At least it was up until yesterday."

"I wonder," Beagle said.

"Wonder what?"

"I wonder how they lifted it out, how they moved it without leaving any marks, what they used to dig it up. I wonder lots of things."

57

"Well, the rest of us are freezing, and I can't see that we're doing any good here."

"Hmm," Beagle said. "Maybe we are."

"Maybe we are what? Would you cut it out, Beagle? Mysterious remarks aren't your style."

"Maybe we are doing some good. Start walking back. I want to check around here some more."

"I just hope the snow will close the roads so the rest of the students can't get back tomorrow," Beth said. "There will be war when they hear about this."

"Maybe it will be found before then," I said, with more confidence than I felt.

"We'll find your cougar," Beagle assured Beth.

"I'm going to tell the others that the whiz kids who found out who took the knife last night are going to find our cougar," Beth said. "Maybe that will cheer them up."

College people are weird, I decided. I could understand Beagle's aunt believing in us, but Beagle had also promised help to the president and now to the students. I didn't think they really took us seriously, but if we didn't find some answers soon, we were going to be very unpopular around Fenster March.

We said goodbye to Beth, and the twins and I

started home. Beagle caught up with us so quickly that I didn't think he could have checked much.

"I found this." He held up a plastic sandwich bag with a sheet of paper inside. "I figured if any clues were left they'd be covered by the snow, so I just dug around a little."

Maybe Charlie was promising more than we could do, but at least he was finding some clues.

We opened the sandwich bag and pulled out a folded slip of paper. Unfolding it, we read:

"OP POF IBT TUPMFO UIF DPVHBS.
XF KVTU NBEF JU EJTBQQFBS."

"Not much help," Beagle said.

"It's code. Let's take it back to your aunt's house and work out what it says."

As soon as we were in the house, I made hot chocolate while Beagle sat at the table and looked at the coded message.

"I think they'd use a pretty simple code," he said. "Somebody wanted this found and read."

"The simplest codes shift the alphabet forward or backward one letter," I said. "O could stand either for P or for N."

59

"Well, PQ is not a word, so let's try shifting all the letters back one."

"So O becomes N and P becomes O. That means the first word is 'NO.' Sounds like a good start."

[To find the message in the coded note, substitute for each letter the one that comes just before it in the alphabet. Check the message you discover against Ellen and Beagle's on the next page.]

Solution to "The Missing Cougar":

When you correctly substitute the preceding letter of the alphabet for each letter in the message, you read: "No one has stolen the cougar. We just made it disappear."

"Great," I said without enthusiasm. "Now we don't have any thieves to catch but we don't have the cougar either."

"You know, it's funny. I don't have any idea what happened to the cougar. But all of a sudden I have a pretty good idea who broke into Aunt Irene's study. I think I'll give the police a call."

.7.

A College Prank from the Past

When Beagle phoned the police station, he learned that his aunt and uncle had already been there talking to a sergeant about the break-in. Beagle spoke to the same sergeant and told him his hunch.

Just as he came back from the phone, Aunt Irene and Uncle Doug arrived with a visitor.

"This is one of our neighbors, Franklin Bevis. His family has been a part of this community for more than a hundred years. We're asking him for his help. Mr. Bevis, this is my nephew Charlie and his friend Ellen."

"Just call me 'Beagle.'"

"Nice to meet you," I said. Making a quick guess, I added, "Are you related to Martin Bevis?"

"Good, Ellen!" Uncle Doug said. "Mr. Bevis is the

only person in our community related to our missing men of 1890. Maybe at least there'll be news of a missing family member."

"Martin Bevis was my great-grandfather and a professor here a century ago. My great-grandmother refused to leave this town because she always believed he would come back; she never believed he was a thief. Irene here has been trying to persuade me to give up some old papers that belonged to him."

"Maybe they would help to prove he wasn't a thief who disappeared with college money," Beagle suggested.

But Mr. Bevis shook his head. "I don't think anyone can figure out the truth after all these years. I can't see what good dragging out an old scandal will do."

Bored by the conversation, the twins left us to go play in the snow. Aunt Irene suggested the rest of us should come out to the kitchen where we could all share hot chocolate.

Sitting with us at the table, Mr. Bevis continued to argue that nothing could be discovered about events many years after they have occurred.

"I remember mysteries from my own college days that have remained unsolved to this day. There's not a chance in the world anybody could figure them out today."

"What sort of mysteries?" Beagle asked.

"Well, things like who stole chickens from old Professor Dubois's hen house and then served them to him at a faculty barbecue? Or, who removed every single chair from Conklin Hall the day before exams were due to begin? Or, who moved some farmer's outhouse onto the college president's front lawn the morning before commencement?"

"There must have been a lot of pranks here when you were in college," I said.

"This school has always had a reputation for pranks," Uncle Doug said. "I hear that we're the victims of the latest one."

"Oh, the stolen cougar," Aunt Irene said. "I haven't had a chance to ask you about that."

"We'll tell you about it later," Beagle said. I could see he had something on his mind, and that usually means work for me. "Mr. Bevis, what if we could clear up some old mystery from your college days; would that change your mind? Would you let us look at the papers you have from your great-grandfather's time?"

Mr. Bevis laughed. "Son, there's not a chance you could figure out something the rest of us didn't know at the time."

"But if we did . . ."

"If you did, I'd say you were as good as Sherlock Holmes, and you could help yourselves to all the information I have."

"Beagle," I said, warningly.

"When were you a student here?" Beagle asked, ignoring my warning.

"I was here from 1947 to 1951," Mr. Bevis said, looking very pleased. He was sure he had us stumped. I decided to do my best to surprise him.

"Pick a mystery, Ellen. I'm going to get some yearbooks."

"Let me tell you about the prank that caused the most trouble on the campus. The year I was a junior I roomed with Ben Sneath, a guy who could never resist a joke. If the officials had only known who was responsible, a prank that year would have ended with at least one boy being expelled. Ben never would tell me all the details of that one, although he knew all about it."

"That would have been 1950, wouldn't it?" Beagle asked coming back into the kitchen with a stack of yearbooks.

"Yes, it would have. I know the three people involved were my roommate Ben Sneath, a youngster named Barston Cole, and Holton Fenwood. The trick was someone in that group turned out the lights during an evening meeting with the dean in the men's dormitory. That dean had no sense of humor and he had been giving all the boys a pretty hard time. I think the plan was to turn the lights out and all of us were going to sneak away and leave him.

"But somebody decided to make the joke even better by dumping a bag of flour over the dean's head just as the lights went out and yelling 'Ghost!' Holton Fenwood always said that he and the person who turned out the lights were the ones who had stolen the bell from the bell tower the year before. And years later I remember Ben Sneath telling me that the person who added the extra touch of dumping the flour used to laugh with him about that prank right up to the time they both graduated."

"That's a lot of facts," I said, taking notes as he talked.

"Maybe, but not enough. I know Ben Sneath couldn't have been the ghost-maker, although he knew who was. But either of the other two could have been. And, while Holton didn't turn off the lights, either Barston or Ben could have. At this late day, no one will ever know."

"I think we'll all know soon," Beagle said, looking up from an open yearbook.

"Look, Ellen. It says here that Ben Sneath was new

to Fenster March that year."

I wrote down the new fact and my list of clues now looked like this:

1. Holton Fenwood and the person who turned off the lights had pulled a prank the year before.
2. Ben Sneath and the "ghost-maker" liked to talk about that night right up until the year they both graduated.
3. Ben Sneath was new to Fenster March that year.

"I'm sure we have enough to solve this mystery for you, Mr. Bevis," I told him after I had looked over the clues. I drew up a chart like this:

	one who turned off lights	ghost-maker
HOLTON FENWOOD		
BEN SNEATH		
BARSTON COLE		

[Before Ellen gives the answer to Mr. Bevis, see if you can work it out for yourself. Remember that the one who turned off the lights was not the ghost-maker. Check your answer against Ellen's solution on the next page.]

Solution to "A College Prank From the Past":

Since Ben Sneath was new to Fenster March, he could not have been involved in a prank there the year before. So clues 1 and 3 together show us that Ben Sneath was not the person who turned out the lights. From the first clue we also know that Holton Fenwood did not turn off the lights. Therefore, the person who turned off the lights must have been Barston Cole. From clue 2, we see that Ben Sneath was not the ghost-maker. Since Barston Cole turned off the lights, he can't be the ghost-maker. Therefore, the ghost-maker was Holton Fenwood.

"Here, see for yourself," I said to Mr. Bevis, showing him the chart while I explained.

"I think you've proved your point," Aunt Irene said.

"How about it, Mr. Bevis?" Beagle asked.

"Yes, I think I'll have to reconsider," Mr. Bevis conceded.

.8.

Beagle's Ghost Story

So far in our visit to Byersville, all we had seemed to do was find more questions to answer: Who had the skeletons been? We knew one of them had a cracked skull, but what had happened to the second one? How had they gotten into the foundation of Hamilton Hall? What had happened to that heavy stone cougar? Why had someone broken into Aunt Irene's office?

At least this time someone else was digging up clues for us. After lunch Aunt Irene and Uncle Doug went out to see what information they could get from Mr. Bevis. Beagle and I stayed with Megan and Lori.

I was glad to be babysitting because it was one way of helping Beagle's aunt and uncle. But we didn't have much time left to solve the mysteries and now the students who were on campus were expecting us to find their cougar.

"Maybe we should be working on the mysteries," I told Beagle.

"Aunt Irene and Uncle Doug will be sure to come back with some new information. We'll make some progress today."

I wasn't sure about that, but I didn't see what we could do other than wait. In a town where we knew so few people and with snow piling up, we couldn't very well go out interviewing people on our own.

"We want to build a snowman," Megan said.

"Why don't we stay inside and tell stories now and build a snowman later," I said.

"Yes, tell us another ghost mystery," Lori said.

"This time it's Beagle's turn," I said. "Let's get him to tell a story."

To a chorus of "yes" and "okay," Beagle had to agree.

"We want a ghost mystery," Lori said.

"I don't know about ghosts, but I'll give you a mystery."

"There has to be a ghost," Megan insisted.

"All right. Sure. One of the characters is a ghost. Now sit down and listen."

We all settled down and Beagle began.

"This is the story of the pirate's ghost. A long time ago, five pirates met on the sandy beach of an island."

"What were . . ." Megan began.

Beagle glared at her and went on. "Their names were Pegleg, Blackcoat, the Red Revenge, Lace Throat, and Laughing Jack. And those were the only names they were ever known by," he added before Lori could ask her question.

"Standing under a coconut palm, fifty paces from a tall, pointed rock, the captain ordered two of the men to dig a deep hole. When it was ready, two others lowered the chest of pirate's gold into it."

"And then what happened?" Lori asked before Beagle could stop her.

"Be quiet, me hearties! Or ye'll never hear the truth of it," he roared threateningly. "The captain drew his musket and shot one of the pirates. 'We'll leave his ghost to guard the treasure,' the captain said."

"Oooh!" Megan and Lori gasped.

Ignoring them, Beagle went on, "So they filled in the hole and sailed away on their ship *The Golden*

71

Harp. But the captain had protected the treasure too well. The ghost was a terrifying one. For many years everyone who came close to the hiding place died, including the captain himself.

"After a while, the last of those pirates died, and today only one person knows the truth of what happened that day—me! If you'd like to know too, then read this note left by the first mate, who was one of the men present, and see if you can find out which man was the captain and which one was the ghost."

The story I had told in the car was made up on the spur of the moment without any thought. Beagle wasn't playing by the same rules. He had worked out a story like mine, except that his was more complicated. He had even prepared the note.

He handed us a ragged paper with brown edges, and this is what Megan and Lori and I saw:

> On this day the captain ordered Laughing Jack to lower our treasure chest onto a boat. I—the pirate known as Lace Throat—together with Blackcoat, Jack, Pegleg, and the Red Revenge put ashore. Blackcoat and Pegleg dug a hole, then stood with me and watched as the captain shot our comrade.
>
> LACE THROAT,
> FIRST MATE OF *THE GOLDEN HARP*

With plenty of comments from the twins, I organized the clues to look like this:

1. The captain ordered Laughing Jack to lower the treasure from the ship to a boat.
2. Blackcoat and Pegleg watched as the captain shot one of the group.
3. First Mate Lace Throat wrote about the killing.

I drew up a chart and the twins helpfully marked in X's and O's while I explained the clues:

	captain	*ghost*
BLACKCOAT		
PEGLEG		
THE RED REVENGE		
LACE THROAT		
LAUGHING JACK		

[Match wits with Beagle and see if you can get the correct answer before checking yourself against Ellen's solution on the next page.]

After we'd solved the puzzle, we all went out to build a snowman. Lori and Megan had already made a start. They had a huge, more or less rounded base for the bottom of the snowman.

"How did you ever make such a giant snowball?" I asked.

"We packed snow around the garbage can," they told me, giggling.

As we began to roll the next snowball, Beagle just stood there, staring at the twins' big garbage-can snowball.

"Aren't you going to help?"

He didn't even hear me. Instead, he said, "That might just be how they did it."

To our amazement, he turned around and started to run.

.9.

A College Prank
of the Present

S eeing Beagle run out of the yard, Lori and Megan
assumed he was playing a new game and ran after
him. I ran after them. As we jogged awkwardly
through the snow, everybody talked.

Lori kept asking, "Where are we going? Where are
we going?"

And Beagle was saying, "Under the snow. That's it.
Down under the rocks and dirt and snow."

"Are you losing your mind?" I called out to Beagle.

"It isn't in the same place. It's right beside itself."

"*You're* beside yourself."

"I'll find it. I know where it is."

"Do we have to run so fast?" Megan asked.

"It's been done before," Beagle said. "They did it at
Princeton. I know. I read about it."

Finally we stopped, right in front of the administration building beside the huge hole that the Polytech students had dug to uproot the Fenster March cougar.

"It's still here," Beagle said. "They never took it. That's how they did the impossible."

"You mean they buried it underground?" I asked staring at the hard reddish ground at the bottom of the hole.

"They made us think they'd moved it, but they didn't move it at all."

I have gotten used to Beagle being selfish, to Beagle promising people that I will do impossible things, to Beagle volunteering me to tell stories, babysit, solve problems. But Beagle talking gibberish was more than I could stand.

"That's enough!" I shouted. "What are you talking about?"

"The cougar," he said, looking at me surprised. "The cougar was never there." He pointed at the hole.

"Are you saying the cougar was an illusion?"

"No, no. The cougar is still here. Right where it always was."

"And where is that?"

"There!" Beagle spun around and pointed to the pile of snow and dirt and rocks that the thieves had dug up. Of course, we all three saw what he meant.

Lori, Megan, Beagle, and I began to dig, to push, to scrabble our way through the heap. And Beagle was right. We soon uncovered the cougar.

Brushing off the last of the snow, we found another plastic bag taped to the cougar's chest.

"There's a note inside," Megan said.

"What does it say?" Lori asked.

We opened it, but this is what we saw:

ENNKDC XNT, CHCM'S VD?
QDUDMFD ENQ ONKXSDBG!
BQTRGDQ & KHFGSMHMF

"Code again," Beagle said disgustedly. "Let's take it home and translate it."

A few minutes later we were back at Beagle's aunt's house. Substituting the preceding letter of the alphabet for each letter of the first line, we got: DMMJCB WMS, BGBL'R UC.

"That's not right!" I said. "Let's try the letter following each letter in the note."

This time the substitution worked, and we began to find real words.

[Decode this second note by substituting the following letter in the alphabet for each letter in the note, and you'll read what Ellen and Beagle found.]

78

"Hey! I know those names," Beagle said when we read the signatures. "They're mentioned in an article I was reading in the school paper while I was cooking breakfast."

"Find it," I urged. "Maybe it will tell us who they are."

In a few minutes we were studying this item from a student newspaper:

> The Polytech Hawks rely heavily on Lomax, Smith, Morris, and Burns. They refer to two of these as "Lightning" and "Crusher" and call them their secret weapons, refusing to reveal which of the four are known by these names.
>
> Burns and Lomax claim that since Lightning joined them last year the average yards gained per play has doubled. Morris boasts of the outstanding tackling ability of both Crusher and Lomax. Smith and Crusher have both been with the team for three years. . . .

"You know, Beagle, I think they may have given themselves away. Maybe we can figure out who these two 'thieves' are before your aunt and uncle get back."

"Yeah, we can tell them about the cougar and who didn't steal it all at once," Megan said.

I made up a list of clues like this:

1. Burns and Lomax told the reporter that Lightning had joined them last year.
2. Morris praised both Crusher and Lomax for their tackling skills.
3. Smith and Crusher have been with the team for three years.

Below the clues, I drew a chart in my notebook:

	Lightning	Crusher
SMITH		
LOMAX		
BURNS		
MORRIS		

[Using the clues above, see if you can solve the puzzle before you check Ellen's answer on the next page.]

"There," I said. "It's about time we found out something to cheer up Aunt Irene."

But just then Aunt Irene and Uncle Doug returned, and I could see from their faces that it would take more than the solution to the missing cougar mystery to make them happy.

"News of the skeletons has leaked out," Aunt Irene said. "The reporters are here. Soon we'll be in headlines all across the state."

.10.

The Bones
in Question

*A*unt Irene was very pleased, after all, to learn how Beagle had found the cougar.

"Good! When the students get back," she said, "instead of just hearing what Polytech did to us, they'll hear how you outsmarted Polytech. That's one story the press can print with my blessing. Now, if only you and Ellen could do something about those skeletons!"

"What did you find out from Mr. Bevis?" I asked. "We're ready to get started."

"Mr. Bevis is still searching for his great-grandfather's papers—or, so he says," Uncle Doug said. "I'm not sure he really wants to share them even though you did meet his terms. I think he's afraid his great-grandfather may really have stolen the donation that disappeared that year. After all, the college was in desperate need of the money and it was rumored to have been a very large sum."

Uncle Doug then said that we should all take time out for supper. And Aunt Irene said that it would have to be steaks and french fries, since she hadn't had time to cook. Beagle told her steak and french fries are his favorite foods. (Of course, it's hard to think of anything that isn't Beagle's favorite food.)

I made a salad, Beagle peeled and sliced potatoes, and the twins set the table. We were all eating when the doorbell rang. Uncle Doug answered it and soon came back with a puzzled look to tell us the police had found a cardboard box full of old papers stuffed into the corner mailbox.

"The papers the thief stole!" Aunt Irene exclaimed.

"Why did he throw them away where they'd be sure to be found?" I asked.

"Maybe he found something he was looking for and threw the rest away," Beagle said.

"Let's take a look," I said, eager to get started. Maybe now we'd find the key to the mysteries.

"The papers can wait. Let's finish eating first," Uncle Doug insisted.

So we ate, but the papers didn't wait long. All of us

knew that time was running out. Soon the weekend would be over, and the snow wouldn't keep the students away for long. In just a few minutes we were all sitting on the floor with papers—clippings, notebooks, letters, old bills, and documents of all kinds—spread around us.

"One thing I've learned from reading these is that the college certainly had a lot of unpaid bills that year. Here are two separate cases when the college was about to be closed and money arrived just in time," Aunt Irene commented after we had spent some time going through papers.

"Where did the money come from?" Beagle asked.

"Mostly private donations. Here's a letter from the college president, who was in the western part of the state where he was asking for donations from families who had helped the college in the past. He's saying he'll have the money soon and to hang on until he gets back."

"In those days," Uncle Doug said, "teachers could go unpaid; but if an institution failed to pay other bills, the sheriff would come and padlock the door."

"Padlocked doors were a real possibility that year," Aunt Irene concluded. "No wonder there was so much hard feeling about the missing money."

"By April of that year," Uncle Doug pointed out, "at least one other person knew about the money that was being donated. If the four men had kept the secret to themselves and then died or left the area that same year, we'd know nothing about it."

"I found something here," Aunt Irene said, "that suggests that one or two of those four men who left the college that year may have been heard from later."

"I think I've found the fifth man," Beagle said.

"I'll make a list of all the clues we've found," I offered.

"I'll make popcorn," Beagle volunteered.

For the next few minutes I wrote while Beagle and Lori and Megan popped popcorn.

Then we all ate popcorn while I shared what we had found out:

1. On a torn sheet of notepaper, I found a plan for five people to keep information about a donation that was being made to the college a secret until they could make a surprise appearance at a ceremony, presenting the money at a dramatic moment to save the college building program.

2. The five men were identified as Pop, Leon-

ard Shutt, Martin Bevis, Stoney, and the treasurer of the building committee.

3. A clipping from the college newspaper said that Pop, Professor Bevis, and the "Great Druid," who headed a secret society on the campus (a society known for its practical jokes) had mysteriously promised to provide the money needed to complete the work on Hamilton Hall.

4. A letter from Leonard Shutt, dated April 12, 1890, addressed to the "Great Druid" mentioned that two people had disappeared attempting to conceal the "secret donation."

5. A memo dated April 25, 1890, and signed "Stoney" was attached to a bill to the college asking the "Great Druid" how they can find new funds now that the donation has disappeared.

"How does all of that help?" Aunt Irene asked. "It's a good thing we already know who Pop and Stoney and the treasurer were, but I don't see what else we can learn from this."

"I think only two of the four men who left the college that year really disappeared permanently. If we can discover which two they were, we should have identified the skeletons."

"Apparently two of the men and the money all disappeared before April 12 of that year," Beagle pointed out.

I decided to use the nicknames "Pop" and "Stoney" in my chart since we knew who they really were, but I substituted Brandon Wells's name for the treasurer. And I drew up a chart to check my clues:

	the "Great Druid"	missing men
LEONARD SHUTT		
POP		
STONEY		
BRANDON WELLS		
MARTIN BEVIS		

[Be careful! This is the toughest of the puzzles Ellen and Beagle have faced. Can you identify the two men who were never heard from after April 12, 1890? To find them you must first identify the "Great Druid." Also pay attention to dates. When you have solved the mystery, check your answer against Ellen's on the next page.]

Solution to "The Bones in Question":

From the third clue, we learn that neither Pop nor Martin Bevis is the Great Druid. The fourth clue tells us that Leonard Shutt is not the Great Druid. Stoney can't be the Great Druid either (clue 5). Therefore, Brandon Wells must be the Great Druid.

Since we know that Leonard Shutt wrote to the Great Druid after the two men disappeared, neither he nor Brandon Wells can be one of the missing men. Because Stoney wrote a letter on April 25, we can eliminate him as a missing man since the two men had disappeared by April 12. Therefore, the two missing men are Martin Bevis and Pop.

"It's a good thing we can identify Pop and Stoney from the work we did earlier," I pointed out. "One of them accounts for one of the skeletons."

"So those are the two who were genuinely never heard of again," Uncle Doug said, looking over my chart.

"The skeletons must be theirs, but why didn't Stoney or this Great Druid person tell people that those two might be dead?"

"There's a simple answer to that," a voice from behind us said.

Startled, we all looked up to find Franklin Bevis standing there.

"I knocked," he told us. "But when there was no answer, I just came on in. I may have found the missing piece of the puzzle."

.11.

The Bare Facts

"**I** heard what you just said about the Great Druid. That was the name given to the leader of a secret society made up of faculty members and occasionally some students. The society was part of Fenster March until 1921. Secret societies were pretty common back then."

"What happened to the secret society?" Beagle asked.

"Oh, the jokes were getting out of hand and the college board's executive committee passed an ordinance abolishing it. But in the 1880s, my great-grandfather was an active member. He was involved in some practical joke just before he disappeared," Franklin Bevis explained.

"Will you show us what you've found?" I asked.

"It's all right here in his diary, but no one ever seemed to realize that the joke led to the disappearance." He held out a worn, old book and asked me to read the last two pages.

"'We are all sworn to secrecy,'" I read, "'but I can say that this will be the most sensational rescue the college has ever known. At the ceremony to lay the cornerstone of the new building, two of us will arrive with the necessary money. One of the college's graduates is giving all we need to save the building program. All he asks is that we don't tell who he is. Just when we thought we would have to stop the building program the money will appear. The coins are gold! What could be better?'"

"My grandfather never let anyone see this diary. He was sure it would confirm the town's suspicion that his father stole the gold," Mr. Bevis told us. "It's obvious my great-grandfather was excited about the gold."

"Yes," Beagle agreed, "but it sounds like he was only glad it was gold because it would make the presentation to the college more dramatic."

"I'm sure you're right. He sounds more excited about helping the college. But with the gold and the men gone, who would have believed that a hundred years ago?"

"There's more from the next day," I said. "'Pop and

91

I have been chosen to present the gold. It will be in our hands tonight. He and I will choose a hiding place to be known only to the two of us. I can't decide among the bell tower, the administration building, the statue of the college mascot, and the black locust tree. Or, maybe we could hide it below the planks covering the excavation for Hamilton Hall itself.' That's the end of the diary."

"That's the last thing he wrote and then he disappeared. You see," Mr. Bevis said, "it was all part of a prank, an elaborate practical joke that went wrong." He looked very sad, thinking of the loss of lives and the grief in his family. "Two lives and the gold were lost, so the secret society wanted to keep its secret. They decided to keep quiet. Maybe they felt guilty. Somehow I hope they did."

We were all silent for a bit, thinking about pranks, about puzzles, about skeletons, and about missing gold. I think at that moment all of us really believed we had learned as much as we'd ever know about what had happened all those years ago.

Mr. Bevis was the first to break the silence. "What I've brought you besides the diary are my great-grandfather's records of the secret society."

"What a good idea," Aunt Irene commented. "I have a separate file of information on the society. I hadn't known it would be involved until tonight. Let me get it."

Looking over Mr. Bevis's notes, we learned that Leonard Shutt and Brandon Wells had gotten their idea for the joke from another member of the group. In the middle of the ceremony to lay the cornerstone of the new building, two people were going to burst out of hiding and lead the assembled group to a hidden treasure. Pop and the planner argued, but later they were friends again.

Going back to her own records of the society during 1890, Aunt Irene found a brief mention of a surprise gift planned for the day the cornerstone would be laid. Apparently someone had approached Brandon and Stoney with the idea of keeping the money and dividing it. They knew the man who was planning the surprise presentation would be furious, so they didn't tell him. Leonard and Brandon thought they had talked the man out of trying to take any of the gold.

"You might as well stick with the nicknames for your notes, Ellen," Aunt Irene said.

My list of clues looked like this:

1. One member of the group had gotten the big idea for the surprise and had told his plan to Brandon and Leonard.

2. Pop and the planner quarreled but later agreed to work together.
3. One member of the group was a would-be thief who'd talked to Brandon and Stoney about splitting the money. None of them wanted the planner to know about the thief's proposal.
4. Without the planner's knowledge, Brandon and Leonard tried to talk the would-be thief out of taking the money.

"That doesn't sound like much information to me," Mr. Bevis said.

"Just watch what Ellen does with it," Beagle said.

I drew up a chart to give it a try:

	planner	would-be thief
STONEY		
MARTIN BEVIS		
BRANDON WELLS		
LEONARD SHUTT		
POP		

[Who planned the surprise presentation of the gold to the college? Who wanted to steal the gold? Use the clues to find your own answers and then check them against Ellen's solution on the next page.]

Solution to "The Bare Facts":

The first clue tells us that neither Brandon nor Leonard is the planner. Pop is not the planner, according to the second clue. And the third clue tells us that Stoney is not the planner either since the thief had talked to him and to Brandon but not to the planner. Therefore, the only person left who could have planned the surprise presentation of the gold to the college was Martin Bevis.

Since Bevis is the planner, he cannot be the thief. Clue 3 reveals that Brandon and Stoney are not the thief. Neither is Leonard, according to clue 4. Therefore, the would-be thief was Pop.

"So that means that the would-be thief and the man who planned the surprise for the college are the two who died," Beagle noted. "If the man who wanted to steal the money is one of the skeletons, what happened to the money?"

"Beagle," I said, "you and your reappearing cougar have given me an idea. What if the money has been here all along? Since it was gold coins, it may even be here still. Maybe it's what Aunt Irene's thief is also trying to find."

.12.

Finding the Gold

*T*he next morning I woke up on my own, without twins bouncing on me. But they heard me and came racing in as soon as I got up.

"We're snowed in," they sang at me.

"Roads are closed. You can't go home."

I looked out the window and decided they had to be right. But I still dressed quickly. That missing gold was bothering me and pushing me to action.

Beagle, it turned out, had the same idea.

"Where's the gold?" he asked me.

"That's just what I've been wondering. And who stole Aunt Irene's records? Maybe the police have checked on your hunch."

"We still have work to do. Let's get going."

"Go? We can't go anywhere," I reminded him.

"Then we'll think it out. We can solve it."

Of course, Beagle didn't intend to start without breakfast. So we headed for the kitchen first. With the twins' help, I made scrambled eggs and toast.

"Doughnuts?" Beagle asked, around a mouthful of egg.

"We don't have any," Megan said sadly.

"I can make some," I told them, "if I can use this package of refrigerated biscuit dough."

The twins popped open the tube of biscuits and I heated oil for frying while they poked holes in the biscuits. After I had fried the dough, they rolled each doughnut in sugar.

Just as we put the plate of doughnuts onto the table, Aunt Irene came in.

"We never did get to hear what you learned from the police about the break-in," I reminded her.

"They have too many suspects and too few clues," she said. "They may never know."

"Hah! That was before I called them with my hunch," Beagle told her.

"What hunch?"

"Oh, Beagle had an idea about who might have taken the things from your office, but I think we'd better not say anything until the police check it out."

When the doughnuts were gone, we all went outside for a while in the deep snow. With Lori and Megan, we tried sledding, throwing snowballs, making angels in the snow. Nothing worked very well because snow was still falling.

"It's lunchtime," Beagle said when we came in. "Let's eat."

"We just had breakfast."

"But it's noon," he insisted.

We'd just finished roast beef sandwiches when someone knocked at the door.

"The police have caught the thief," Uncle Doug told us a few minutes later. "It was Rocky Marshall. They say Charlie gave them the tip."

"Are they sure?" Aunt Irene asked.

"He still had one of the 1890 papers with him. Besides, he admits it."

"But what made you suspect him, Charlie? Why would he do it?"

"For the same reason he took the knife that was found with the skeleton," Beagle said. "He's trying to solve a mystery too, only in his case the mystery has been the missing gold all along. Am I right?"

"He says there have always been rumors about gold lost on the campus. He claims he meant to find it and give it to the college," Uncle Doug said. "Should we press charges for the break-in?" he asked Aunt Irene.

"I'd like to talk to Rocky first. I can't believe he meant to do anything but provide us all with a surprise. Apparently this college has had a tough time with people who plan surprises. Of course, he gave us quite a scare even if all he really meant to do was find the missing treasure for the college," Aunt Irene said.

"Did the police return the paper Rocky had kept?" I asked, hoping we were close to the end of the mysteries of skeletons, break-in, and missing gold.

"Yes, it's right here. Rocky said he couldn't make any sense of it and was going to return it anyway."

We all crowded around to read the old sheet of paper.

Pop,
    Meet me at the administration building, and we will go from there to our hiding place. Since the Great Druid has agreed to leave this to us, we'll keep him separate from us and the treasure by having him give a signal from the bell tower. You and I will be able to see the bell tower from where we'll be

99

hidden, but the cougar statue will be between us and the building site, so we'll need a
signal to know the right moment in the ceremony.

The two of us will lead everyone past the
administration building to the hidden treasure.

"This ought to tell us where they put the treasure,"
Aunt Irene said.

"I think it will, with the help of one of Professor
Bevis's diary entries," I said.

"I remember the one you mean," Beagle said.
"You're thinking of the list of possible hiding places
that Dr. Bevis mentioned. They were the black locust
tree, the bell tower, the administration building, the
cougar statue, and under the planks covering the excavation site at Hamilton Hall. Right?"

"That's right," I agreed and set to work with pencil
and paper.

"We never tried to identify a place before," Beagle
pointed out. "How do we do this?"

"It's still just a matter of logic and elimination. It
ought to work," I told him. "Here, look at the clues."

1. Pop and Dr. Bevis were going to walk from
the administration building to the place

100

where the two of them were planning to
hide.

2. The Great Druid was going to be in the bell
   tower, separate from both the treasure and
   the two men in hiding.

3. At a signal from the bell tower, the men
   would come out of hiding and go to
   Hamilton Hall. From there they would lead
   the crowd past the administration building
   to the hidden treasure.

4. From their hiding place, they would be able
   to see both the cougar and the bell tower.

"I see, but I don't get it, if you know what I mean,"
Beagle said.

"Help me. I think we will get the answers."

Using a chart to mark off clues, we sorted out the
information.

	the men's hiding place	hidden treasure
ADMINISTRATION BUILDING		
BLACK LOCUST TREE		
HAMILTON HALL		
COUGAR		
BELL TOWER		

[Where were the men planning to hide? Where was the treasure to be hidden? The men were not going to hide in the same place that the treasure was to be hidden. You will first need to know where the men were to hide in order to find where the gold was hidden. When you have found your answer, check it against Ellen and Beagle's solution on the next page.]

Solution to "Finding the Gold":

The first clue makes it clear that the men were not planning to hide in the administration building. They would also not be hidden in the bell tower or at Hamilton Hall (clue 2). From clue 3, we learn that they cannot be hiding behind the cougar. Therefore, their hiding place is the black locust tree.

Since the treasure is not with the men, it is not at the black locust tree. It is also not at the administration building since the men will lead everyone past it to the treasure. Of course, it isn't at Hamilton Hall either since they are going to lead people from the building site to the treasure. The treasure is not at the bell tower either (clue 3). So the treasure must be hidden at the cougar statue.

"But the cougar is impossible to move!" Beagle said.

"A hundred years ago it wouldn't have been so deeply sunk into the ground," I pointed out. "Two men could have tipped it over and back without anyone knowing."

"Then Pop killed Professor Bevis to claim the gold for himself?" Beagle suggested.

"Perhaps he didn't mean to kill him," Uncle Doug said. "He may only have intended to knock him out; but, when he did kill him, he tried to hide the body. The police have discovered that the second skeleton had a broken neck. Pop probably fell to his own death when he dropped the professor's body into the excavation for the new building."

"You two are terrific detectives. I knew you could do it," Aunt Irene said, beaming at me and Beagle.

"How did you know we could solve the mysteries?" I asked. "We didn't even know ourselves."

"The Beagle Detective Agency always solves the case," Beagle said. "Everybody knows that."

"If you two are correct," Aunt Irene said, "the gold may still be here, right where Professor Bevis hid it back in 1890."

Beagle and I grinned. That was what we had been saying.

By midafternoon, the snow stopped and we cleared the walk and driveway, but we still couldn't drive home from Byersville.

"Resign yourselves to missing a day of school," Uncle Doug told us.

Resign ourselves? Missing school might mean that we would still be here when they searched for the gold!

104

Aunt Irene spent most of the time on the phone and at supper she reported to us.

"There are teams out right now clearing snow from around the cougar. The construction company has agreed to excavate the base and use the crane that's already on the building site to lift the cougar tomorrow."

"It's pirate's gold," Lori said.

"What about the ghost that's left to guard it?" Megan asked.

"In this case I think he'd want us to have it," I assured them.

On the next day they found the gold, which was a better discovery than the bones had been. And there were plenty of reporters on hand to take pictures.

My favorite picture was the one of Beagle and me beside the cougar with the open chest of gold in front of us. There were also pictures of the president shaking our hands, of me looking into the ruins where the skeletons were discovered, and of Beagle with his arm around the neck of the cougar he'd found.

Aunt Irene made sure the reporters knew the whole story. The headlines said:

HIDDEN TREASURE DISCOVERED AT
FENSTER MARCH
Young Sleuths Solve Century-Old Mystery